AURORA
Means Dawn

by Scott Russell Sanders / illustrated by Jill Kastner

Bradbury Press   New York

Bradbury Press
An Affiliate of Macmillan, Inc.
866 Third Avenue, New York, NY 10022
Collier Macmillan Canada, Inc.

The text of this book is set in ITC Berkeley Old Style.
The illustrations are watercolor paintings reproduced in full color.
Typography by Julie Quan

Printed and bound by South China Printing Company, Hong Kong

First American Edition
10 9 8 7 6 5 4 3 2

LIBRARY OF CONGRESS CATALOGING-IN-PUBLICATION DATA
Sanders, Scott R. (Scott Russell), date.
Aurora means dawn / by Scott Russell Sanders; illustrated by Jill
Kastner. — 1st American ed.
     p.   cm.
Summary: After traveling from Connecticut to Ohio in 1800 to start
a new life in the settlement of Aurora, the Sheldons find that they
are the first family to arrive there and realize that they will be
starting a new community by themselves.
ISBN 0-02-778270-0
[1. Frontier and pioneer life — Fiction.   2. Ohio — Fiction.]
I. Kastner, Jill, ill.   II. Title.
PZ7.S19786Au 1989   [Fic] — dc19   88-24127 CIP AC

For Mia, Naomi, Julia, and Lara
——S.R.S.

For my mother, with love
——J.K.

When Mr. and Mrs. Sheldon reached Ohio in 1800 with seven children, two oxen, and a bulging wagon, they were greeted

by a bone-rattling thunderstorm.
The younger children wailed.
The older children spoke of returning to Connecticut.

The oxen pretended to be four-legged boulders and would budge neither forward nor backward, for all of Mr. Sheldon's thwacking. Lightning toppled so many oaks and elms across the wagon track that even a dozen agreeable oxen would have done them no good, in any case.

They camped. More precisely, they spent the night squatting in mud beneath the wagon, trying to keep dry.

Every few minutes, Mrs. Sheldon would count the children, touching each head in turn, to make sure none of the seven had vanished in the deluge.

Mrs. Sheldon remarked to her husband that there had never been any storms even remotely like this one back in Connecticut. "Nor any cheap land," he replied. "No land's cheap if you perish before setting eyes on it," she said. A boom of thunder ended talk. They fell asleep to the roar of rain.

Next morning, it was hard
to tell just where the wagon track
had been, there were so many
trees down.
　　Husband and wife tried
cutting their way forward.

After chopping up and dragging aside only a few felled trees, and with half the morning gone, they decided Mr. Sheldon should go fetch help from Aurora, their destination.

On the land-company map
they had carried from the East,
Aurora was advertised as a
village, with mill and store and
clustered cabins. But the actual
place turned out to consist of a
surveyor's post topped by
a red streamer.

So Mr. Sheldon walked to
the next village shown on
the map—Hudson,

which fortunately
did exist,
and by morning
he'd found eight men
who agreed to help
him clear the road.

Their axes flashed for hours in the sunlight.
It took them until late afternoon

to reach the wagon.

With the track cleared,
the oxen still could not move the
wagon through the mud until
all nine men and one woman
and every child except the toddler
and the baby put their shoulders
to the wheels.

They reached Aurora at dusk, making out the surveyor's post in the lantern light. The men from Hudson insisted on returning that night to their own homes. Ax blades glinted on their shoulders as they disappeared from the circle of the campfire.

Huddled together like a basketful of kittens, the children slept in the hollow of a sycamore tree. Mr. and Mrs. Sheldon carried the lantern in circles around the sycamore, gazing at this forest that would become their farm. Aurora meant dawn; they knew that. And their family was the dawn of dawn, the first glimmering in this new place.

The next settlers did not come for three years.

A NOTE FROM THE AUTHOR

▼ ▼ ▼ ▼ ▼ ▼ ▼ ▼ ▼ ▼ ▼ ▼ ▼ ▼

I grew up on the back roads of Ohio, not far from the towns of Aurora and Hudson where this story takes place. Traipsing through the countryside, I often wondered what it must have been like for the early settlers who cut the first roads, built the first log cabins, cleared the first farms in this territory. (The Indians had long since occupied the land, of course. But they did not count in the eyes of the white pioneers, however much they may count in ours.) What lured the pioneers from the civilized East to the wild forests of the West? How did they get on with the woods, the Indians, the animals, the outlaws, and one another?

My speculations on these matters eventually found their way into fifty brief tales, which were collected a few years ago into a book called *Wilderness Plots*. Each of the tales, including "Aurora Means Dawn," which I have retold here for children, grew from a seed of fact: a diary, a soldier's log, a letter, a newspaper clipping, or some other historical account. I never had much to go on—perhaps a name, a haunting phrase, or a colorful gesture—just enough to give me a tantalizing glimpse into a vanished life.

In writing "Aurora Means Dawn," I knew only that Mr. and Mrs. Job Sheldon and their seven children had been caught within a few miles of their destination by a terrible storm; and that Aurora, far from being an established village as they had been led to expect, was an unbroken woods. I love thunderstorms, and I love swinging an ax, and I love sycamores, so everything else in this tale was a pleasure to imagine. I saw the lightning-struck trees felled across the path, the oxen mired in the mud, the family sheltering under their loaded wagon. I saw them delivered, first by their own labors and then with the help of neighbors. I lay with the children in the hollow tree, and at the same time I circled about that tree with the parents, feeling their mixture of fear and ache and excitement.

This is how I, at least, lay hold of history: by imagining my way back into past lives.

—Scott Russell Sanders